Balloons G

Story by Beverley Randell
Illustrations by Liz Alger

Rigby

A Harcourt Achieve Imprint

www.Rigby.com
1-800-531-5015

"The green balloon is for me,"
said Nick.

"The blue balloon is for me,"
said Kate.

"Here is a red balloon

for me," said James.

"Look at my balloon,"

shouted Nick.

"My balloon is up in a tree."

Pop!

"Oh no!" said Nick.

"My balloon

is up in a tree, too,"

shouted Kate.

Pop!

"Oh no!" said Kate.

James said,

"**My** balloon

is not going to pop."

"Here comes my red balloon!"

said James.